1.4.2000

To Dearest [illegible]

Wishing You A Very Happy

Birthday.

Love,

Bali

THE BANANA
ROBBER
AND OTHER STORIES

The Banana Robber

and Other Stories

by
ENID BLYTON

Illustrated by
Suzy-Jane Tanner and Peter Wilks

AWARD PUBLICATIONS

For further information on Enid Blyton please contact www.blyton.com

ISBN 0-86163-914-6

This edition entitled *The Banana Robber and Other Stories*
published by permission of The Enid Blyton Company

This edition first published 1998

Published by Award Publications Limited
27 Longford Street, London NW1 3DZ

Printed in Hungary

CONTENTS

1 The Kitten that Disappeared   7

2 The Three Sailors   15

3 Pippitty's Joke   28

4 Tig and Tag   40

5 Dame Poke Around   47

6 The Foolish Green Frog   58

7 Hello Rabbit   70

8 The Bear Who Lost His Growl   88

9 The Little White Hen   99

10 The Fire in the Nursery   110

11 That Tiresome Brownie   116

12 The Easter Chickens   132

13 Annabelle's Little Thimble   140

14 The Poor Little Owl   151

15 The Banana Robber   161

16 The Doll with Straight Hair   172

17 Lost Baby Mouse   182

CONTENTS

The Rocking Horse

1

The Kitten That Disappeared

John and Rosie had a kitten of their own. It was three months old, as black as coal, with eyes as green as a cucumber. It was the merriest, lovingest, warmest little kitten you can imagine, and the two children loved it with all their hearts.

It was called Fluffy, and it always came when it heard its name. It was very mischievous, and loved to hide under the beds or under the chairs and pounce out at peoples's toes. Fluffy loved every one and every one loved Fluffy.

And then one day she disappeared. It was the most extraordinary thing. One minute she was playing with the two children in the kitchen and the next minute she was gone!

Mother was busy. It was Monday morning and she had a lot to do. She had washed up. She had done the laundry and put the dirty sheets and

8

towels into the big basket for the
laundry man to collect. She had made
the beds and peeled some potatoes for
dinner. And all the time Fluffy had
played about with the children, sometimes jumping up at Mother, sometimes
trying to catch her apron-strings as she
whisked here and there.

Then she was gone!

'Mother, where is Fluffy?' said Rosie,
looking round.

'Hiding somewhere, I expect,' said
Mother, fastening up the laundry basket
in a hurry because she heard the
laundry man coming down the passage.

'Fluffy, Fluffy!' called John – and
there came an answering mew from
somewhere, very tiny. 'MeeOOOOO!'

'She's somewhere!' said John, and the
children began to look under the dresser
and under the stove. The laundry man
rang the bell, and Mother gave him the
laundry basket. She shut the door so
that Fluffy shouldn't run out if she were
hiding somewhere. John called again.
'Fluffy! Fluffy!'

9

But no matter how he listened he couldn't hear another mew. No – Fluffy didn't answer at all. Rosie hunted under the bottom shelf of the broom cupboard, and then in the cupboard where the newspapers were kept. But Fluffy wasn't anywhere to be found!

'Oh, Mother, Fluffy has quite, quite disappeared!' said Rosie, almost crying.

'Don't be silly, darling,' said Mother. 'She must be somewhere about. She is hiding. Perhaps she has slipped upstairs and gone under one of the beds.'

'But, Mother, the kitchen door has been shut all the time,' said John. 'She simply must be in the kitchen if she is anywhere.'

'Well, she'll turn up all right,' said Mother. 'Don't worry. I haven't time to help you hunt now, but when I've finished making this pudding for your dinner I will have a look round. But I expect by that time that Fluffy will come dancing out from somewhere!'

But do you know, she didn't! So when Mother had finished making the pud-

10

ding and popped it into the oven to cook, she had a look round for Fluffy too. She put down the saucer of milk and fish for the kitten, and called her.

'Fluffy, Fluffy, Fluffy! Puss, puss, puss! Dinner, dinner, dinner!'

But still no Fluffy came dancing out on black, velvety paws! Rosie cried big tears.

'Mother, it's magic! Some fairy has taken Fluffy away!'

'Nonsense, darling!' said Mother, laughing. 'The fairies never do unkind things. Fluffy may be in the garden.'

So they put on their coats and hunted all round the garden. No Fluffy. They went to the house next door, but Mrs. Brown hadn't seen their kitten at all. They went to Mrs. White's too – but she hadn't seen Fluffy since the day before.

Well, the children hunted and called all morning, but Fluffy was not found. They had their dinner, and then hunted again.

'Never mind,' said Mother. 'Fluffy will come in when she is hungry.'

'Mother, I don't think she ever went out,' said John. 'I don't really. One minute she was playing hide-and-seek with us, and the kitchen door was shut, I know – and the next minute she had disappeared.'

Although Mother put a saucer of fish and milk in the garden as well as in the kitchen, no Fluffy came to eat it – and Mother began to get worried too. She was very fond of the little black kitten and she could *not* think where it had got to. But at last she knew!

There came a ring at the kitchen door. Mother went to open it – and there was the laundry man, grinning all over his red, cheerful face. In his hand he held a box.

'Good afternoon, Mrs. Jones,' he said. 'I just wanted to tell You that you had sent

12

this to the laundry, but as it seems quite clean, we wondered if you really *did* want it washed!'

He opened up the little box he carried – and in it, curled up, was Fluffy! How the children shouted and danced for joy! Mother stared at Fluffy in astonishment.

'Whatever do you mean?' she asked the man.

'Well, Madam, when we opened your laundry basket at the laundry, we found this little black kitten fast asleep inside!'

13

'Good gracious!' said Mother. 'She must have jumped inside when she was playing hide and seek with the children – and I didn't notice her – and shut down the lid! Then you took the basket away with Fluffy inside! We did hear a faint mew from somewhere – she must have been in the basket then!'

How glad Fluffy was to see the children again! How she pranced and danced on her four paddy-paws! How she licked up her fish and milk! How she mewed and purred! What a fuss was made of her!

'Oh, Mother! Fancy sending our kitten to the laundry!' said Rosie. 'Suppose she had been washed and ironed, whatever would she have thought!'

It's a good thing the laundry *didn't* wash, and iron Fluffy, isn't it! She *did* have a narrow escape!

2

The Three Sailors

Tom, Joan, and Eric were staying by the sea. Their house was almost on the beach. It was lovely. Every day they had tea on the beach, and Granny, Mother and Daddy came too.

Granny didn't like sitting on the sand to have tea, so Daddy had brought down a wooden table from the house for her. Mother had a tablecloth, and Granny sat up at the table and poured out tea and milk for everyone.

After tea the children wanted to go out in a boat.

'No,' said Daddy. 'Not today. I want to finish my book. Besides, the sea is too rough today. You wouldn't like going in a boat.'

'Oh, Daddy, we should, we should!' said Tom. 'We are such good sailors. Can't we go in a boat by ourselves? We could manage it quite all right.'

16

'Certainly not!' said Daddy. 'It would never do at all.'

So the children had to be good and dig castles in the sand. Granny helped them. She gave them bits of coloured wool too, to put among the seaweed for flowers when they made a garden for the castle.

'Perhaps Daddy will take you in a boat tomorrow,' she said.

The next day the sea was just as rough, but the children ran to ask their Daddy to get a boat.

'No, my dears, the sea is still too rough,' Daddy said. 'You might be sea-sick.'

'Oh, Daddy, we wouldn't be, really and truly!' said Eric. 'We are such good sailors. Do take us! Oh, do get a boat and let us go out in it!'

But Daddy wouldn't. He said they could none of them swim well enough to go out in a boat on a rough sea.

'I'm sure I could swim all right if I fell out of a boat,' said Joan, sulking.

'Oh, I do want to go.'

17

Then Daddy got cross and said nobody was to mention boats again till he did. So the three children set to work to dig, though they all looked rather sulky.

It was Granny who thought of a good idea for them. 'Why don't you turn the wooden table upside down and pretend it is a boat?' she said. 'That would be fun. You could tie the table cloth to Daddy's stick and tie that to one of the table legs – and you would have a mast and sail! Your spades can be oars.'

'Oooh, yes! We'll play pirates!' cried Eric in excitement. 'Come and help, you others.'

So in a trice the table was turned upside down, and Eric began to tie Daddy's stick to a leg for a mast. Then Joan tied the table cloth to the stick, and the wind flapped it out for a fine sail. Really, it was most exciting!

'Daddy and Granny and I are going for a walk this afternoon till teatime,' said Mother. 'We will bring tea down with us when we come back. Amuse yourselves well and have a nice afternoon, all of you.'

The three children were left on the beach alone. They were pleased. Now they could play pirates and shout all they wanted to. What a fine boat the big wooden table made!

They got the cushions out of the chairs in the house and put them in the upside-down table. They got their spades for oars. The sail flapped merrily in the breeze.

19

'Yo-ho for a life on the ocean wave!' shouted Tom. 'We'll have some fine adventures!'

They did! They sailed after ships and caught them. They took prisoners. They had a wreck. They did enjoy their game – and at last they were so hot and tired that they didn't want to play any more.

'I'm going to have a rest,' said Tom, flopping down on a cushion in the upside-down table.

'So am I,' said Joan, fanning herself.

'Let's pretend that we are drifting off to a wonderful treasure island!' said Eric. 'Ship your oars, every one! Whilst we rest, our ship will take us to a wonderful land where we can find hidden treasure.'

They all lay down on the cushions and shut their eyes. The sun shone down. It was lovely and hot. The little breeze cooled them nicely. In two minutes all three children were fast asleep.

Now the tide was coming in very fast, with the wind behind it. A big wave ran right up the beach and lapped against the table. The children didn't see it. They were fast asleep, of course. Another wave came, and another. Each one ran up to the table. A bigger wave still ran all around it.

Then such a big wave came that it lifted the table up! It was floating! Two more waves ran under the table – and then, whatever do you think! The waves took that upside-down table and floated it gently out to sea.

Eric's feet were in the water but he didn't notice it. Joan's hair hung over the side of the table and got wet, but she was fast asleep. Tom's spade floated off by itself.

The sea was pleased with its boat. It bobbed it up and down, up and down – and suddenly a wave splashed right over the table and woke all three children up with a jump!

They sat up in a hurry. How astonished they were to find themselves out at sea on their table! The beach looked a long, long way away!

'Oooh! Our table's a real boat!' said Tom, looking scared.

'The sea has taken it away!' said Joan.

'We wanted to go out in a boat by ourselves and now we have,' said Eric, not liking it at all.

'I feel sick,' said Tom, holding on to the table, for it was bobbing up and down tremendously on the waves.

'So do I,' said Joan.

'I feel frightened,' said Eric, beginning

to cry. 'We can't swim enough to save ourselves.'

'I told Daddy I could, but I daren't,' said Joan.

'Oh, what shall we do?' wept Eric. I'm afraid – I'm afraid!'

The three poor sailors clung to the bobbing table for all they were worth. The tablecloth sail flapped merrily. The cushions were soaked every time a big wave broke on the table.

'We shall all be drowned!' said Tom, looking very white.

'If only someone would rescue us!' cried Eric, his tears tasting as salty as the sea-spray.

'Look! There's Daddy coming down to the beach with the tea things!' said Joan.

'Yell as loudly as you can,' said Tom.

So they yelled, 'Dad-dee, Dad-dee, Dad-dee!'

Their father was looking round the beach in surprise, seeing no children. Then he suddenly heard their voices and looked out to sea. How astonished he was to see the three sailors on the table!

'Save us, Daddy, save us!' shouted Tom.

Do you know what Daddy did? He began to laugh and laugh!

'So you are three sailors after all!' he shouted. 'How do you like it?'

'Oh, Daddy, save us!' shouted Joan.

'You silly children, jump into the water and wade to the shore with the table!' yelled Daddy.

'Daddy, we shall be drowned!' wept Eric. 'The sea is so deep!'

'Tom! Jump out and wade to shore!' shouted Daddy again. 'Go on – do as I tell you. I'm not going to wet my nice white trousers to come and fetch you in.'

Tom put one leg over the table into the

sea. He clung hard to the table-leg and let himself go into the water. Splash!

What a surprise for him! Although he was so far out from shore the sea was only up to his knees. It took a long time for the sea to get really deep at their seaside, for the tide flowed in over level sand.

'Oh! We can paddle back,' said Tom in surprise. 'I'm only up to my knees. Get out, Joan, and help.'

Joan jumped out. Then Eric jumped

too - and together the three sailors paddled back to the beach, dragging their table behind them.

'Well, well, well!' said Daddy, still laughing. 'Who's going to worry me to take them out in a boat on a rough sea again?'

Nobody said a word. Nobody wanted to go out in a boat on the rough sea now. The three sailors were rather ashamed of themselves.

But Granny and Mother were quite excited to hear about the adventures, so they all cheered up, put the table the right way up for Granny, and had a lovely tea.

Weren't they funny? I would have loved to see them sailing away fast asleep on their upside-down table, wouldn't you?

3
Pippitty's Joke

Pippitty was a pixie – but what a naughty one. The things he did! He stuck a stamp on the pavement, and watched every one trying in vain to pick it up! He put a parcel in the gutter, and when the passers-by bent to see what it was it suddenly jerked away and made them jump – for Pippitty had got a black thread tied to it, and he was holding the other end round the corner.

When he got caught by Mother Go-Along, she spanked him so hard that he cried a whole bucket of tears.

'I'll pay you out for this spanking!' said Pippitty, and he ran off home. When he got there he wondered how he could play a trick on Mother Go-Along without her knowing that it was he who was doing it.

And at last he thought of a joke. 'I'll fly up to her roof – and take a can of water with me – and sit by her chimney – and pour water down it on to her fire! Then it will sizzle and smoke and she'll think some one has put a spell on it and will be so frightened!' chuckled naughty Pippitty to himself. Wasn't he a monkey?

Well, he waited till night came. Then up to the chimney he flew, carrying with him a big can of water. He knew which was the kitchen chimney, for smoke was coming from it. My word, Mother Go-Along must be having a good fire, for the smoke was simply pouring out!

Pippitty grinned to himself. He sat on the edge of the chimney and tipped up the heavy can of water. Splishy-splashy-splishy-splashy – it hurried down that sooty chimney to the fire below!

Mother Go-Along was sitting in her rocking-chair by the fire, knitting peacefully. Suddenly, as a trickle of water reached the flames, the fire gave a loud sizzle-sizzle, sizzle, and sent out a cloud of black smoke!

'Good gracious!' said Mother Go-Along in alarm, 'What's all this?'

She poked the fire – it burnt up again after a while, so Mother Go-Along sat down once more to do her knitting. Flames shot up the chimney.

It was nice and warm.

Pippitty, sitting up on the roof thought it was time to send down another lot of water – so he tipped up the can. An extra big lot went down – splishy-splashy-splishy-splashy! It reached the fire.

SIZZLE-SOZZLE-SIZZLE-SOZZLE!' What a noise the fire made when the water tried to put it out! Mother Go-Along jumped up in fright. Clouds of dark smoke billowed out into her kitchen.

'It's a spell someone has put on my fire!' she cried. 'Yes – a spell!'

She cried this out in such a loud voice that Pippitty heard it, up on the roof. He grinned and chuckled and nearly fell off the chimney in delight. Aha! This was a fine punishment for Mother Go-Along! That would teach her to spank him! Oho!

31

He tipped up the can and sent down another lot of water – but this was too much for poor Mother Go-Along. When the fire said, 'Sizzle-sozzle,' again she ran out of the door squealing. 'Help! Help! There's a spell on my fire!' she cried.

Pippitty laughed so much that he fell right off the chimney and nearly slid down the roof. He decided to wait and see what would happen. Presently Mother Go-Along came back with Dame Quick-Eyes. Pippitty could hear them talking.

'I tell you there's a dreadful spell on my fire!' said Mother Go-Along. 'It keeps shouting "Sizzle-Sozzle" at me, and sending out clouds of black smoke.'

'Dear, dear,' said Dame Quick Eyes. 'Well, we must see what we can do about it!'

They went indoors. Pippitty put his ear to the chimney to hear what they said. He still had a little water left in his can. What fun to give Dame Quick-Eyes a fright too.

32

The fire was out. Dame Quick-Eyes
told Mother Go-Along to make another.
So in a few minutes sticks were burning
merrily, and a nice fire roared up the
chimney. The two dames sat down to
see if the spell would work again.

33

They didn't have to wait long! Pippitty tipped up his can – splishy-sploshy-splishy-sploshy – down went the water, rushing through the chimney to the fire.

'Sizzle-sozzle-sizzle-sozzle!' shouted the fire and a cloud of smoke blew out! Dame Quick Eyes had quick ears as well as quick eyes, and she had heard the splashing sound of the water – and she had seen, too, the wetness that came around the hearth before the heat dried it up. *Some*one, yes, *some*one was pouring water down Mother Go-Along's chimney! Ho ho! So that was it!

Dame Quick Eyes whispered to Mother Go-Along. 'I'll catch the one who's doing this! Have you got a butterfly-net or a fishing-net anywhere about?'

'I've got an old fishing-net in the cupboard,' whispered back Mother Go-Along. 'I'll get it. Whatever are you going to do?'

She fetched the net. Pippitty, who had his ear to the chimney, couldn't hear a word. He was longing to know if he had frightened Dame Quick-Eyes too!

Dame Quick-Eyes was busy – very busy! She had stolen to the door and opened it. She had rubbed a spell on the fishing-net to make it bigger – and bigger – and bigger! It grew so long that it was higher than the roof! And then Dame Quick-Eyes looked up to the chimneys – and, very faintly indeed

36

against the cloudy night sky she spied someone sitting on the chimney! Aha!

She held up her long, long net – she held it just over the chimney – she brought it down on the chimney – smack! And she caught Pippitty!

What a surprise he got when that net came down on him! He jumped so much that he almost fell down the chimney himself! He couldn't get out of the net, however much he struggled.

Dame Quick-Eyes twisted the net round, with Pippity inside, and brought it down to the ground. She made the net smaller in a trice, put out her hand and grabbed Pippitty.

'So it's you, is it, you monkey!' she said. 'I might have guessed it!' She took the frightened pixie in to Mother Go-Along, who stared in surprise.

'Pippitty sat up on the roof and poured water down your chimney,' said Dame Quick-Eyes. 'That was what made the fire say "Sizzle-sozzle," and made the black smoke too. Do you want to spank him again Mother Go-Along?'

On no, don't spank me!' begged Pippitty. 'Anything else but that!'

'Spanking's no good for a naughty pixie like that,' said Mother Go-Along. 'I've tried it once – and see what happened. He just came and poured water down my chimney. No, Dame Quick-Eyes, I shall do something better than that. You said he was a monkey, so he shall be! When he's tired of being a real one, I'll turn him back into a Pixie again and see if he can behave himself!'

She muttered three magic words over Pippitty – and in a trice he turned into a little brown monkey with big brown eyes and a long tail. What a shock for him that was!

He scurried away out of the cottage to hide himself. What *would* his friends say when they saw him? Oh dear, oh dear!

'He behaved like a monkey, and now that he is one he ought to be pleased,' said Dame Quick-Eyes.

But he wasn't! The funny thing is that now he *is* a monkey he doesn't

38

behave like one – he behaves like a perfectly good pixie! I expect Mother Go-Along will change him back to his own shape soon – but if you happen to see a small monkey anywhere about with soft brown eyes, have a good look at him. It may be that rascal Pippitty!

4
Tig and Tag

Tig and Tag were two quarrelsome brownies. My goodness, how they squabbled! Sometimes it was really funny to hear them, because they shouted at one another for half-an-hour on end.

One day they went to fetch a basket of apples from Dame Twinkle. She had so many that she had said she would spare some for them.

They took the basket from Dame Twinkle and thanked her politely. Then off they went home. On the way they met Snick and Snack, the two gnomes.

'Spare us an apple each Tig and Tag,' said Snick looking longingly at the basket of rosy apples.

'No!' said Tig and Tag at once, both together. They were mean little creatures, and never gave anything away if they could help it. They went on, scowling. Snick and Snack winked at one another.

'If we can make them quarrel, we can take the apples for ourselves without Tig or Tag noticing,' said naughty Snick.

So they followed close behind the two brownies till they came to the hill that went up to the town.

'Look!' said Snick in a loud voice. 'Tig is letting Tag carry most of the weight of the basket! Isn't he mean! Up the hill too, just when they should both help fairly.'

Tag heard what Snick said and he stopped and glared at Tig.

'Snick says you are making me carry most of the weight,' he said. 'Please be fair, Tig, and carry your side of the handle properly.'

41

'I am!' shouted Tig.

'You're not!' shouted Tag.

'Now they're off!' whispered Snick to Snack. 'We can get close and take an apple or two without either of them noticing. Once they start to squabble they forget everything except their quarrel.'

'Yesterday you made me carry most of the washing-basket when we took it to - Dame Feefo's!' shouted Tag.

'I didn't!' roared Tig.

'You did!'

'I didn't!'

'I say you did!'

'And I say I didn't!'

'Don't yell at me like that!'

'I'm not!'

'You are!'

'I tell you I'm NOT!'

'And I tell you you ARE!'

'You'll be sorry you spoke to me like this!'

'No I shan't!'

'You will!'

'I won't!'

Snick and Snack grinned as they listened. They took two apples each from the basket. The quarrelsome brownies didn't notice. Some small pixies came up, and, seeing Snick and Snack helping themselves from the basket, they helped themselves too, standing and eating the apples whilst they watched Tig and Tag quarrelling.

'You're a long-nosed cucumber, that's what you are,' said Tig to Tag very rudely.

'And you're a red-faced tomato!' shouted Tag.

'I'm not!'

'You are!'

'I'm not!'

'Oh, be quiet!'

'Well, be quiet yourself!'

'I shan't!'

'Nor shall I!'

'You want smacking!'

'So do you!'

'I don't!'

'You do!'

So the two quarrelsome brownies went on, squabbling hard, till quite a crowd came round them. And everyone helped themselves to apples and stood munching round, watching. Tig and Tag didn't notice anything.

'I'll carry the apples home myself without your help,' said Tig.

'And I'll carry them without yours,' said Tag.

They both rushed for the basket – and dear me, you should have seen their faces when they found it was empty! They stared round at all the crowd eating apples, and they shook their knobbly fists in rage.

'You've taken our apples!'

'Well, they were there,' said Snick. 'You didn't seem to want them, either of you. You shouldn't quarrel so. Then you could keep an eye on what belongs to you.

'I hope you'll all have a pain in your tummies!' shouted Tag to everyone. And picking up the empty basket the brownies went sadly off home, making up their minds never to quarrel again. But you know, I'm afraid they will.

As for Snick and Snack and the rest, they did have pains in their tummies, which really served them right, for they shouldn't have taken those apples.

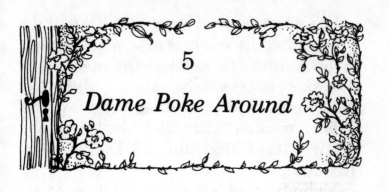

5

Dame Poke Around

Old Dame Poke-Around came out of her cottage with her bag. She locked the door, put the key in her pocket and went to catch the bus to the next village. She was going to stay with her sister, Goody Grey-Hair.

The folk of Apple Village were glad to see Dame Poke-Around going away, even if it was only for a few days. They thought she was a mean, nosy old woman. She would never give a penny to any one, nor even a bun to a hungry child. And she was always poking around, trying to find out things that people wanted to hide.

She knew when Dame Flip-Flap had a hole in her shoe. She knew when Mister Twink had forgotten to post Mrs. Twink's letters. She knew when the little boys and girls over the way had been smacked and put to bed. Oh, she knew everything, did old Dame Poke-Around.

Nobody had ever known her to do anything to help anyone. When Dame Flip-Flap lost her purse of money just at Christmas-time all the folk of the village joined together to give her the money she had lost – all except Dame Poke-Around. She said Dame Flip-Flap was a careless creature and deserved to lose her purse, and *she* wasn't going to give her a penny.

And when little Lucy Locket had whooping cough badly, and had to be sent away to the seaside to get better, the village folk all gave fifty pence each to help her to pay for the journey – all except for Dame Poke-Around, and she said Lucy Locket was making a fuss and didn't need a change at all.

So you can see that nobody minded when Dame Poke-Around went away for a week or two! The children especially were glad to see her go, for she scolded them whenever they played near her cottage.

Dame Poke-Around arrived at her sister Goody Grey-Hair's and settled in. She took the best bed and the biggest helping of everything, but Goody Grey-Hair was kind and generous and did not mind. Before Dame Poke-Around had

been there three days, there came a knock at the door.

Goody Grey-Hair opened it. Outside stood a little brownie with a notebook, and pencil and a big purse.

'Please,' he said, 'I'm collecting.'

'What for?' asked Goody Grey-Hair.

'Well, a house has been burnt down in the next village,' said the little brownie.

'It belongs to an old woman, so we are all trying to get some money to pay for the house to be mended.'

'Dear, dear!' said Goody Grey-Hair. 'How sad! Well, I'll get my purse.'

'Oh no, you won't,' said Dame Poke-Around, coming to the front door. 'You won't give a single penny to the brownie. Is it a house in Apple Village that has been burnt down, Brownie?'

'Yes,' said the brownie.

'Well, that's the village that *I* come from,' said Dame Poke-Around, 'and I can tell you there's not a single person there who doesn't deserve to have their house burnt down! Whose house was it, Brownie?'

'I don't know,' said the Brownie. 'I belong to this village – I was told to collect money here for this old woman whose cottage was burnt down in Apple Village. All I know is that it was a grey cottage with roses at the door.'

'Hoo! That would be Dame Flip-Flap's!' said Dame Poke-Around joyfully. 'Well, she deserves her bad luck. Careless, lazy creature – always has holes in her shoes, and her hair flopping about her face! You just go and give all the money back that you've collected, Brownie, and tell people that the person you've collected for isn't worth it! The idea of mending up Dame Flip-Flap's old house for her! I shouldn't be surprised if she burnt it down on purpose!'

'Well, of course, if the person isn't worthy of having help, then I shall not collect money for her,' said the brownie, and off he went to give back the money he had already taken from kindly folk of the village.

Dame Poke-Around was delighted to think she had stopped people from

giving money to help Dame Flip-Flap.
She talked about nothing else all the
time she stayed with Goody Grey-Hair,
and really, her sister was quite glad
when at last her stay came to an end,
and she could see Dame Poke-Around
off on the bus to her home!

Dame Poke-Around rode in the bus to
Apple Village. She got off and walked
up the street to her cottage. She had a
look at Dame Flip-Flap's house to see
how badly burnt it was – and to her
great surprise it wasn't burnt at all!
How strange!

But Dame Poke-Around got an even greater surprise when she came to her *own* grey cottage – for that was almost burnt down to the ground! Yes – the windows were gone, the roof was gone, and the front door was black and scorched. The walls had great holes in them – it was a dreadful sight!

'Oh! Oh! I forgot that my cottage was a grey one too – with roses at the door,' said Dame Poke-Around, in horror. 'It's mine that is burnt! Oh dear! Oh dear! Whatever shall I do?'

She ran to Bron's, the chief brownie's,

and asked to see him. 'Oh, Bron!' she cried. 'My cottage is burnt down! What shall I do? I have no home – no money!'

'That is so,' said Bron, looking very grave.

'Won't the villagers help me?' cried Dame Poke-Around.

Bron shook his head. 'Dame Poke-Around,' he said sternly, 'when we knew your cottage was burnt, we went from house to house asking people to give money to help you – and my cousin who lives in the next village, said he would ask people there. But when he came to your sister's cottage, and told the news, *you* thought it was Dame Flip-Flap's cottage that had been burnt – you said a great many unkind things. So my cousin gave back all the money he had collected and came to tell me why. And when I knew that it was *you* who were being so mean – you, for whom we were collecting so much money – why then I gave back all the money that *I* had collected! So there is none for you, Dame Poke-Around. Good-day.'

The old woman had the door shut in her face. She went down the street, weeping, and wondering what she should do. How foolish she had been! How mean! It was herself she had been mean to – and how horrid it felt!

As she passed Dame Flip-Flap's house the door opened and the kindly old woman looked out.

'Dame Poke-Around! I'm sorry your house was burnt down. You can come and stay with me a night or two if you like.'

'But I said such horrid things about you,' wept the old dame.

'Oh, never mind that,' said Dame Flip-Flap. 'You're in trouble and that's all that matters!'

So Dame Poke-Around went to stay with Dame Flip-Flap, and my goodness me, didn't she learn a lot of things there – kindliness, cheerfulness, pity, generosity – it's no wonder she was a different person when she left the kindly dame and went to earn money to pay for the mending of her house!

And now the first one who opens her purse to any one in trouble is Dame Poke-Around. A good thing too, isn't it.

6

The Foolish Green Frog

There was once a green frog who used to float in Peter's bath every night. He was a nice little toy frog, and he and the toy goldfish swam together for Peter and made him laugh.

One day, Peter took the toy frog out into the garden with him. He played with it for a little while and then he threw it onto the grass. When it began to rain he ran indoors and left the frog by itself.

The frog didn't like the rain. It was afraid its nice green paint would come off. So it hopped away under a bush. And there it met a big thrush, turning over some moss to hunt for snails.

'Hallo!' said the thrush in surprise. 'What are you doing here, little frog?' I thought all good frogs lived in ponds in the springtime.'

'Is that so?' said the little frog. 'Well, I will certainly go to live in the pond, too.'

'Shall I show you the way?' asked the thrush, politely. 'You are not very big so perhaps you are not old enough to know the way.'

'I can find it by myself, thank you,' said the frog, haughtily. 'I am quite big enough. Good-bye!'

He hopped off to look for the pond. He longed to be a proper frog and not a toy one. He wanted to play with other frogs and have a good time.

But he didn't really know what the pond was like, so after a bit, when he met a garden snail he stopped and spoke to him.

'Good-day,' he said, 'could you tell me if I am anywhere near the pond?'

'Well,' said the snail, looking all around, 'that looks like it over there, doesn't it!'

The snail pointed with his horns to a large puddle on the path. The snail was very small so to him the puddle was as large as a pond. The frog took his word for it and at once leapt over to the puddle. He lay down in it, hoping that very soon he would see one or two real frogs to play with. But he didn't.

The sun came out and shone warmly, and very soon the puddle began to dry

The Foolish Green Frog

up! Then the frog found himself lying on a dry path, and the thrush,who came flying by at that moment, laughed loudly.

'Did you think that puddle was the pond?' he cried. 'Oh, you funny little fellow! That was only a puddle, and now it is dried up, so if you don't move someone will come along and tread on you!'

The frog hopped off quickly, angry with the laughing thrush. Soon he came to a big old sink, lying on the ground full of water. The gardener had put it there for the hens to drink from, but the little frog felt sure it was a pond. So into the old sink it hopped and swam around looking for more frogs to play with. But he didn't find any.

Soon, along came two big hens to have a drink, and they clucked loudly when they saw the little green frog.

'A frog in the drinking-water! Think of that! Let's drink him up!'

They pecked at the frightened frog, but he sprang out of the old sink and

hopped away. One hen hit him with her beak and made a dent in his shoulder. He didn't like it at all.

On and on he went, and at last came to a big rain-barrel into which dripped water from the roofs. Beside it was a worm, poking his head out of a hole.

'Good-day,' said the frog. 'Can you tell me where the pond is?'

'What is a pond?' asked the worm, in wonder, for he had never left his little

hole in all his life.

'Oh, it's a lot of water,' said the frog.

'Dear me, then, that must be the pond in this great barrel you see,' said the worm. 'I once heard the robin say that it was full of water.'

'Thank you,' said the frog, and you should have seen him making his way up the side of the barrel! It was quite exciting to watch him, and the worm felt certain he would tumble off and bump his head on the ground. But he didn't. He reached the top in safety and dived into the water that filled the barrel.

There were no other frogs there. It was most disappointing. The little toy frog swam about and then he suddenly saw a big face looking at him . It was the cook, coming out to get a pail full of water from the rain-barrel, and she *was* surprised to see a frog there!

He was so frightened that he leapt straight out of the rain-tub and fell to the ground.

'What are you doing in our rain-barrel!' cried the cook. Then he knew

that he hadn't been in the pond after all. On he went again – and at last he really did come to the pond!

But it wasn't the frog-pond, no it was the duck-pond! No frogs live in duck-ponds for the ducks eat every one that they find. But the little toy frog didn't know that. He was so anxious to be a real, proper frog that he didn't think of any danger, but jumped head-first into the duck-pond and swam about to find some friends to play with.

But the only creatures there were the big white ducks! They saw him, and thinking he was a real live frog, they all came swimming up.

'Here's a frog!' they quacked. 'Here's a frog! Let's eat him! Oh, what a fine morsel!'

The frog was frightened almost out of his life! He must run away quickly before these big white birds pecked him and swallowed him. Out of the pond he jumped and all the ducks waddled out of the water after him.

Then suddenly something swooped

down on him from the air and snapped
him up – and off he went into the air to
the sound of flapping wings! At first he
thought the duck had caught him, but
soon he heard a chuckle and knew that
it was the thrush who had offered so
politely to show him the way to the
pond.

'Well,' said the thrush, 'you've made a
pretty mess of things, haven't you? I've

watched you, and how I've laughed! I saw you in a puddle, and I saw you nearly drunk by those hens. I watched you climb into the rain-tub and how I chuckled when you sprang into the duck-pond! I was just in time to rescue you!'

'Oh, thank you,' said the little green frog gratefully. 'I'm sorry I was rude to you at first. Where are you taking me to?'

'Well don't you want to go to the frog-pond?' asked the thrush.

'Not now,' said the frog. 'I've learned my lesson. I'm not a real frog and I never will be. I'm only a toy frog and I'd better try to be what I'm meant to be – something for a little boy to play with. Will you take me back to Peter?'

'You'll just be in time for his bath!' said the thrush. He flew in at the open window and dropped the frog from his beak. Splash! He fell into a bath of warm water, and a little voice cried out: 'Oh, look! Here's Froggy back again! Oh, wherever did he come from!'

It was Peter, having a bath! He *was* so pleased to see the little frog, and as for the toy gold-fish he nearly went mad with joy to see his friend once more.

'I shall never try to be grand again,' thought the toy frog, swimming happily in the bath. And as far as I know, he swims each night there still!

7
Hello Rabbit!

'There's a new boy coming to school to-morrow,' said Bob to Timothy. 'I heard Miss Smith say so. Perhaps he will be jolly good at running and jumping, and we can have good games with him.'

'His name's Peter Jones,' said Timothy. 'He has come to live next door to us – but I don't think much of him, Bob. We do want a good runner and jumper, you know, to play leapfrog and that sort of thing. There are too many girls at this school! We want a few more boys!'

So Bob and Timothy looked closely at
Peter when he came to school the next
day. He had rather a pale face, sandy-
coloured hair, and his legs were very
thin. He didn't look as if he would be
much good at anything, really.

At playtime the two boys went up to
Peter. 'Come on, Peter!' said Bob. 'Let's
have a game. Race you round the
playground!'

'Well,' said Peter, 'I'd love it – but I
can't run very fast.'

'Well, do your best,' said Timothy.
'Now then, one, two, three, go!'

Off went the three – but before they
had gone very far, Peter stopped, and
leaned against the wall to watch the
other two.

'I can't run any farther,' he said when they came up to him.

'Well, you *are* a poor runner,' said Bob. 'Come on, let's play leapfrog.'

72

'I can't jump very well either,' said Peter, but he tried to leap over Bob when Bob went down. Over he went – and down he fell, knocking Bob over too.

'I told you I couldn't jump!' he said. 'I'm sorry, Bob – but I did tell you!'

'You *are* a rabbit!' said Bob, picking himself up, and glaring at Peter. 'Fancy not being able even to play leapfrog. You're no use to *us*!'

Peter went very red and turned away. Soon the school bell rang, and they all went in, boys and girls together.

At dinnertime Bob and Tim put on their coats and called to Peter.

'Coming along with us, Rabbit?'

'No, I'm going to stay at school for dinner each day,' said Peter.

'Whatever for?' cried the two boys in surprise.

'My mother says it's too far for me to walk home and back again twice a day,' said Peter.

'Poor little sandy Rabbit!' said Bob, mockingly. 'Diddums then! Were his poor little legs too tired!'

'I do think you are horrid,' said Peter, and he turned away.

'Well, good-bye, Rabbit!' called Bob, and off went the two, chuckling together. Peter went in to school dinner, very much wishing that he could have gone off with Bob and Tim. He would like to have told his mother all about his new school but he would have to wait until teatime.

'What a silly little rabbit,' Bob said to Tim on the way home. 'Can't run! Can't jump! Too far to walk home! Let's call him Rabbit, shall we, Tim?'

'Yes, it's a good name for him,' said Tim. So Rabbit became Peter's name, and soon everyone in the school caught hold of the nickname, and wherever he went, Peter heard the same thing: 'Hallo, Rabbit!'

He was good at school-work and his teachers were pleased with him. He never minded helping anyone else, and the girls and some of the younger boys liked him very much. But Bob and Tim still laughed at him, and tried to make

him race with them just for the fun of seeing him stop and say, 'I can't!'

On the day of the school sports all the boys and girls were very much excited. There were to be running races, jumping, three-legged race, egg-and-spoon race and an obstacle race. What fun!

'You must all be here at half-past two,' said the teacher. 'The sports begin at three, and your parents will be here then.'

75

So every one came at half-past two, and went into the sunny field, where Miss Smith had lists of the races and was telling every one what to do.

'I'm in for every single race!' boasted Bob. 'How many are you in for Rabbit?'

'I'm not going in for anything this year except the egg-and-spoon race,' said Peter. 'My mother says I can go in

for everything next year.'

'Poor old Rabbit!' said Bob. 'Poor dear old spindle-legs! Was he afraid of falling over then? Won't the spoon be too heavy to carry?'

'I wish you wouldn't be so horrid,' said Peter, and he went red and walked away.

'Good-bye, Rabbit! sang out Tim. But Peter didn't answer.

The sports were great fun! And who do you suppose won the egg-and-spoon race? Why, Peter did! The spoons were very small and the eggs were rather big – so most of the boys and girls dropped theirs – but Peter's hand was very steady, and although he ran very slowly indeed he managed to get to the winning-post before anyone else.

'Well, you needn't boast about your winning *that* feeble race!' said Bob. 'It's a girl's race, *I* always think! Girls have to do such a lot of sewing and knitting and they're used to keeping their hands steady! I wouldn't want to win that race!'

At the end of the sports all the childen cheered their teachers, their parents and the school. Then they took their prizes and went home. Bob and Tim had seven prizes between them, so they were delighted.

'Look at this!' said Bob to Peter, and he showed him a brand-new purse. 'I won that for the long jump. And the prize for the high jump was fifty pence and I won that too – so I have put the fifty pence into the purse, and I am going to spend it all on my mother's birthday next week! What do you think of that?'

'Won't your mother be pleased!' said Peter. 'I hope next year I'll win some money too– because my mother's birthday is in a fortnight's time.'

'Well,' said Tim, 'It's time we went home. Come on, Bob. I suppose you won't come with us, Rabbit – we are going to run.'

'No, I'll come by myself,' said Peter. 'Goodbye.'

Off went Bob and Tim and Peter walked slowly behind them, down the

80

long street. Soon Bob and Tim were out of sight – and how Peter wished he could run as fast as they could! He would soon be home then!

As he turned the corner, he saw something lying in the gutter. He went to pick it up – and what do you suppose it was? Why, it was the fine new purse that Bob had won at the sports! Peter opened it – yes, there inside was the fifty pence too! Bob must have dropped it without knowing as he ran home.

'He *will* be upset!' thought Peter to himself. 'I wonder if Tim would take it round to Bob this evening after tea. I could slip in next door and ask him. Then Bob would know that his purse and money were safe.' So after he had had his tea, Peter ran to the house next door, where Tim lived, and asked for Tim. When Tim came, he told him about the purse he had found.

'Poor old Bob! He will be upset when he gets home and finds he's lost it,' said Tim. 'Well, you can give it back to him at school tomorrow.'

'I wondered if you'd like to take it to him tonight,' said Peter. 'He might be worrying about it.'

'Oh, I can't do that,' said Tim. 'I'm tired after all those sports. I've got a nice new book and I'm going to read it and have a quiet time. Bob won't mind waiting till tomorrow.'

Peter went back to his house, and looked at the purse. He knew quite well that Bob would be worrying very much over his lost money. Bob was fond of his mother and loved nothing better than to give her things, and do things for her. Peter guessed that he had been making all sorts of fine plans about spending his fifty pence on his mother's birthday.

'I've a good mind to take the purse round to him myself,' thought Peter. 'It's a pity he lives so far away – right at the other side of the steep hill. But perhaps I can catch a bus back. I've still got my last week's pocket money!'

His mother was out, so Peter told the maid where he was going, and set off. It certainly was a long walk, but at last the little boy reached Bob's house. He walked up the path and knocked at the door. Bob's mother came – and she said Bob was in the garden. So Peter went through the house and sure enough, there was Bob, sitting on a seat, looking as gloomy as could be. Peter thought he looked as if he had been crying for his eyes were red – and he guessed it was about the lost purse. He *was* glad he had brought it back to Bob!

'Hallo, Rabbit!' said Bob, in the greatest astonishment. 'Whatever have you come for?'

'Bob, I found your purse with the fifty pence in,' said Peter, and he held it out to Bob. 'I knew you'd be worrying, so I brought it back for you. Here it is.'

Bob took it, a big smile coming over

his face at once. He went red with delight, and shouted for joy.

'Three cheers! I thought it was gone for good! I say, Rabbit it *is* nice of you to bring it back! You can't think how glad I am! I've been worrying about it all the time!'

'That's all right,' said Peter. 'Now I must go, Bob because I'd like to catch the bus back.'

'Did you walk here?' asked Bob.

'Yes,' said Peter.

'Well, I'd never have thought you would have done that!' said Bob, in surprise. 'It's such a long way. And you aren't any good at running or things like that.'

'Well, you see – ' said Peter, and then he stopped.

'Well, what?' asked Bob.

'Well – I broke my leg last autumn – and I can't seem to run and jump as I used to,' explained Peter. 'But my mother says if I take things easily, and don't try to do too much, I shall soon be able to do everything well again.'

85

Bob stared at Peter – and went very red indeed. He had never felt so ashamed of himself in his life! To think they had teased and jeered at Peter because he couldn't run and jump – and it was all because he had had a broken leg!

'Rabbit, I'm terribly sorry that Tim and I were so horrid to you,' he said. 'We didn't know.'

'You didn't give me a chance to tell you,' said Peter. 'Besides, I hate making excuses. I knew that I should be able to run and jump as well as you can in time. So I waited.'

'You're a real sport!' said Bob, and he flung his arm around Peter. 'Will you be our friend? We always wanted a good sport to join us in our walks and games. Will you forget our horridness and be friends?'

'I'd love to!' said Peter, his face shining. 'My, won't we have some fine times together! You can come and play with my steam-train. I've been longing to show it to you. Oh, we'll have great times together.'

'And we won't call you Rabbit any more!' said Bob.

'Oh, but I like it!' said Peter. 'I don't mind it a bit. I know I'm not a real rabbit, you see – someone really feeble and weak. I'll be as strong as you are soon! Call me Rabbit all you like – *I* don't mind!' So Peter is still Rabbit – and now you should see the three of them together! They are the very best of friends, and Peter's legs are getting stronger again. I shouldn't be at all surprised if he beats the other two at the sports next year – but *they* won't mind. They will cheer and say: 'Well done, Rabbit!'

8

The Bear Who Lost His Growl

There was once a big, handsome, toy bear on wheels who had a most lovely deep growl. At the back of his neck was a little brass ring and if you pulled this, he always growled, because the ring worked his growl inside him.

Beppo the bear was very proud of his growl. It was so loud and deep that all the other toy animals used to jump when they heard it. It sounded as fierce as could be, but Beppo wasn't fierce –

he was the nicest, kindest old toy bear you could wish to see.

He belonged to Juliet and she loved him very much. She would sit on his back and get her mother to pull her round the room. Every now and again she would pull the brass ring and make the bear growl.

One day she had a little boy to tea. Goodness, but wasn't Jimmy rough! He pulled half the doll's golden hair off,

and broke a cup and a plate belonging to the doll's tea set. And then he suddenly saw the toy bear! 'Ho!' he said, in delight. 'Come on, Juliet! I'll get on his back and you can pull me round the room!'

So Juliet pulled him round and round the playroom, though she really thought Jimmy was too heavy to sit on her little toy bear. He soon found that by pulling the brass ring he could make the bear growl, and he pulled and pulled it. The poor bear got quite tired of growling!

His voice got hoarser and hoarser, and at last he had none left at all. He couldn't even whisper a growl! Then Jimmy became angry and he pulled so hard at the brass ring that it suddenly broke off in his hand!

'Oh dear!' said Juliet, with tears in her eyes, 'now the bear won't be able to growl any more! You've broken his brass ring!'

'Pooh, he wouldn't growl even before the ring was broken!' said Jimmy.

'Only because you used up his nice deep voice, with making him growl so often,' Juliet said crossly.

'Now, children, don't quarrel,' said Mother. 'Put your toys away, Juliet. It's time for Jimmy to go home.'

That night, when all the toys awoke and crept out of the toy cupboard, the big bear was very sad.

'What's the matter, Beppo?' asked the grey furry cat, who squeaked if you pressed her middle.

'Plenty,' said Beppo the bear. 'I've lost my growl.'

'What can we do about it?' asked the jumping kangaroo. 'Can we buy another one?'

'I've never heard of growls being sold,' said the fairy doll, shaking her head.

'Well, I simply must get a growl from somewhere!' sighed the big bear. 'I wonder whether any other animal that growls would lend me his growl.'

'Dogs growl,' said the jumping kangaroo. 'I've heard them.'

'What about Rover next door?' said the wooden soldier suddenly. 'He has a very fierce growl indeed. He might let you have it if you asked him. He has a bark and a whine too, and I expect he could quite well do without his growl.'

'Well, he wouldn't give it to me for nothing,' said the bear. 'What could I give him for it?'

'He loves sweets,' said the wooden soldier. 'Let's take him some sweets from the toy sweet-shop. The shop-keeper won't mind.'

So in great excitement all the toys went to the toy sweet-shop and begged for a packet of sweets and chocolates from the cardboard shopkeeper. He gave them what they wanted, neatly packed

in a paper bag. Then, with Beppo the bear, they started off to find Rover, the dog next door. The toy bear was so big that he took them all on his back, and they did enjoy the ride!

When they got to Rover's kennel, he barked a welcome, for he was very fond of toys. They told him about Beppo's lost growl and showed him the sweets they had brought.

'You have a bark and a whine, as well as a growl,' said the jumping kangaroo. 'Will you give Beppo the bear your growl, if we give you all these sweets?'

He opened the paper bag and showed Rover the sweets. He sniffed at them and, dear me, how he wanted them!

'Well,' he said, 'I don't mind parting with my growl at all – it really isn't much use to me. My bark is what I use most. But I don't know how I can give it to Beppo. It's inside me, and I don't know how to get it out.'

'Oh,' said the fairy doll. 'I know what we can do about that! There's a funny little brownie woman who lives under the hawthorn hedge just outside the garden. She is very kind and clever and I'm sure she could manage to give your growl to Beppo.'

Then Rover and all the toys went to find the wise brownie woman. She was sitting inside her little house, hidden well under the hawthorn hedge, spinning wool on her spinning-wheel. She peeped out at the toys and listened to all they had to say.

'Yes,' she said, 'I can manage to do what you want. Rover, please growl loudly.'

So Rover growled, and the brownie woman cleverly caught his growl as it came from his throat and wrapped it into a morsel of rice-paper. She pressed it into a round pill and put it into a tiny glass of water.

'Now, Beppo,' she said to the bear. 'Drink this, and swallow the pill with the water.'

So Beppo drank up the water and swallowed the pill. It went down his throat beautifully.

'Now try to growl,' said the brownie woman.

Beppo tried – and oh, would you believe it, he had the deepest, fiercest growl you ever heard!

'Ha!' said Beppo, delighted. 'It's a finer one than I had before! Thank you, brownie woman, and thank you, Rover. I feel quite happy again!'

They took Rover back to his kennel and gave him the bag of sweets. He was pleased! They left him eating them one by one, and they all rode back home on Beppo's back. He growled to make them shiver with fright!

'Oh, don't do that!' cried the fairy doll. 'You'll make me fall off, really you will!'

When the cock crowed they were fast asleep. In the morning Juliet took her toys from the cupboard.

'Poor, poor Beppo!' she said. 'Your growl is broken, and I am so sad!'

'Gr-r-r-r-r-r!' growled Beppo, just like a dog growls, and Juliet squeaked in delight. She threw her arms round her bear's neck and hugged him.

'How did you get your growl back?' she cried.

But Beppo wouldn't tell her. All he said was 'Gr-r-r-r-r-r!'

9

The Little White Hen

Once a little white hen came wandering into the garden belonging to Snip and Snap, the brownies. They were surprised and pleased.

'We'll try and find out where she belongs, and if we can't, we'll keep her for our own,' said Snip.

So they asked everyone in the village if they knew whose the little white hen was, but nobody knew at all. So Snip and Snap kept her.

'We'll make her a dear little hen-house out of a wooden box,' said Snip.

'And we'll put a little nest of hay in one corner for her to lay her eggs in,' said Snap.

'And she shall be called Snowball,' said Snip.

'That's a silly name for a hen,' said Snap. 'That's a cat's name.'

'Well, call her White-Feathers then,' said Snip.

So they called her White-Feathers, and threw down some corn for her to peck up. She ran to it with loud clucks and pecked it all up in a few minutes. Then she went into the box that Snip and Snap had set ready for her, and sat down on the hay in the corner.

'She's going to lay us an egg,' said Snip, delighted.

'I shall have it for my breakfast,' said Snap.

'No, you won't!' said Snip at once. 'I shall have it for my tea.'

'Cluck!' said the hen, and got off the nest. And there, in the middle of the

hay, was the prettiest brown egg you ever saw. The brownies stared in delight. Snip stooped down and got out the egg. It was smooth and warm in his hand.

'Thank you, White-Feathers,' he said. 'Thank you very much!'

The brownies looked at the brown egg with joy. This was marvellous!

'Snip, this hen will bring us luck!' said Snap. 'If she lays an egg every single day, we can sell some of them. We could sell three of them at ten pence each. That's thirty pence a week. We could have the other four for ourselves. What shall we do with thirty pence a week?'

'Save it up and buy a little pig!' said Snip. 'I've always wanted a pig. They look so round and fat and comfortable. Yes – we'll buy a pig.'

'And the pig will grow simply enormous, and we'll sell it and get a lot of money!' said Snap. 'My goodness, we shall be rich! We might get ten pounds for the pig. What shall we call the pig, Snip?'

'We'll call him Roundy,' said Snip. 'That's a good name for a pig. Well, what shall we do with the money that we get for the pig?'

'We'll buy a cow, and we'll call her Mooey,' said Snap. 'And we can milk

102

her each day and sell the milk. Snip, we shall soon be rich! Fancy that! What shall we do with all our money? We'll have bags and bags of it.'

'Well, we'll buy ourselves new suits of silver and gold,' said Snip.

'And we'll build a new house with a hundred windows and sixty chimneys,' said Snap.

'And I'll have a horse and carriage that will go *trit-trot, trit-trot*, all through the town, and make people stare like anything,' said Snip.

'Oh no!' said Snap at once. 'Not a horse and carriage, Snip. That's very old-fashioned. We'll have a bright red motor-car with yellow wheels, and a horn that goes *honk-a-honk-honk*. Then everyone will jump quickly out of the way!'

'Everybody has a motor-car,' said Snip. 'I want to be different. I want a horse and carriage. And my horse shall be called Clippity-Clop. And when it goes along its hoofs will say its name all the time – *clippity-clop, clippity-clop.*'

'No, Snip,' said Snap. 'I tell you we'll have a motor-car. Don't you want to go *honk-a-honk-honk* and make everyone rush out of the way?'

'No, I don't,' said Snip. 'And, anyway, I can make people get out of the way with a horse and carriage, can't I? I can whip my horse and make him go like the wind. And what is more, Snap, if I see you coming along I'll gallop him straight at you and make you jump on to the pavement!'

'Oh, will you?' cried Snap. 'Well, let

me tell you this, Snip – when I've got
my motor-car I'll drive round the town
till I see you coming, and I'll honk my
horn so loudly that you'll drop all your

shopping, and then I'll drive my red motor-car at you, and run you over – *bang, bump*!'

'You horrid, unkind thing!' said Snip in a trembling voice. 'If you do that, I'll gallop right over you with my horse and tell him to kick you away to the moon.'

'You won't, you won't!' cried Snap. 'Look – here I come at you with my motor-car – look out!'

The angry little brownie pretended that he was in a car, and he rushed at Snip, making a noise like a horn – *honk-honk-honk*!

'Well, you look out too, then!' shouted Snip, and he pretended he was riding on a horse. He galloped at Snap, and the two brownies bumped together so hard that all their breath went. Snip fell over, *bang*!

He jumped up in a great rage. He still had the egg in his hand and he thought it was a stone. He threw it hard at Snap. But it missed him – and the egg sailed through the air and flew straight at White-Feathers the hen, who

was listening to the quarrel, quite frightened.

Blip! The egg hit her hard on the beak. It broke, and the yellow yolk streamed out and fell to the ground. White-Feathers gave an angry cluck.

'Cluck, cluck, cluck! If that's the way you treat my nice brown egg, I won't stay with you! Cluck, cluck! Goodbye!'

107

And she spread her pretty white wings and flew right over the fence. Off she went, flapping and running, and the two brownies stared after her in great surprise.

'Come back, White-Feathers, come back!' called Snip, big tears rolling down his cheeks.

But she didn't come back. Goodness knows where she went!

108

'There goes our hen – and Roundy, our nice little pig – and Mooey, our dear cow – and our horse and carriage and bright red motor-car with yellow wheels,' wept Snap.

'And we've lost that nice little brown egg too,' sobbed Snip. 'I'm sorry I was so silly, Snap. Do forgive me.'

'I will, because I'm sorry too,' said Snap. 'Oh, why did we spoil our piece of good luck? Never mind, Snip – next time a white hen comes into our garden, we won't quarrel and lose her!'

But so far no white hen has come again. Isn't it a pity? It just shows how silly it is to quarrel, Snip and Snap!

10

The Fire in the Nursery

One night, after everyone had gone to bed, a hot coal rolled out of the nursery fire on to the rug. There was a lot of smoke as it burnt the rug - and then suddenly a little flame came, and the rug flared up!

The clock struck twelve - it was midnight. At once all the toys came alive and sat up.

'Fire!' shouted the Teddy bear. 'Quick! Where's the toy fire engine?'

110

It rushed up – but there was so little water in the firemen's pails that the fire could not be put out. It ate up the rug – and then the flames went to a wooden chair and began to burn that too!

'The house will be burnt down!' wailed the dolls. 'Golly, Teddy, go and wake up everyone. Run quickly!'

But the nursery door was tightly shut! Alas! Not one of the toys was tall enough to open it. Whatever could they do?

'It will burn the dolls' house next!' cried the clown. 'Oh my, oh my, if only we could reach the tap!'

But no one could climb up to the nursery basin – and even if they had, their tiny fingers were not strong enough to turn the big tap.

'I know, I know!' shouted the toy engine, running along the floor out of reach of the flames. 'Let us all make a great noise and perhaps we shall wake everyone up!'

'Good idea!' cried the toys. 'Teddy, you are the biggest. You beat the drum!'

So Teddy beat the drum loudly – rum-ti-tum-ti-tum! And Golly got the whistle and blew it – pheeeeee! The big doll set the humming-top going hmmmmmm! All the clockwork toys were wound up and they jigged about for all they were worth. The sailor doll took a tin tray from the dolls' house and banged with a toy spoon. Really, you never heard such a noise!

Belinda, who was asleep in the night nursery next door, woke up with a jump. What could that noise be? She slipped out of bed and opened the nursery door – and then, how she stared and stared! The toys were leaping about, shouting, beating the drum, banging the tray, the top was humming, the whistle was blowing – and oh, oh, oh! The room was on fire!

'Mummy, Daddy, quick! Fire! Fire!' shouted Belinda – and in a trice the grown-ups rushed into the nursery, and very soon there was water all over the place! It was thrown over the flames, and the fire was put out in two minutes!

'What a narrow escape!' said Mummy, looking pale. 'Belinda, darling, how did you know there was a fire? Did you smell it?'

'No, Mummy,' said Belinda. 'The toys must have known about it and wanted to wake me – because I heard such a noise, and when I got out of bed to see – well, you should have seen all the toys! They were as alive as could be, jumping and shouting, and . . .'

'Oh, no, Belinda, you must have dreamt that!' said Mummy – and no one would believe her.

But Belinda knows it's true – and so do the toys. As for the drum, there is a big hole in it because the bear banged it so hard that night. But nobody minds – and Belinda showed the hole to me, so I know what happened, you see!

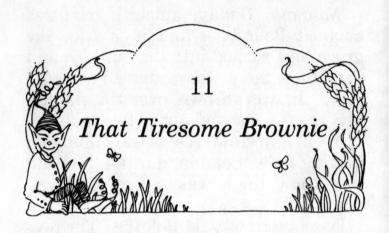

11

That Tiresome Brownie

Farmer Straws was very angry.

In his dairy there was a hidden brownie, and try as he would, the farmer could not find out where he was hiding.

'He sips my cream at night, drinks the milk, licks the butter and nibbles at the cheese!' raged Mister Straws. 'That tiresome brownie! Wait till I catch him!'

A little chuckle came from somewhere in the dairy, and the farmer glared round him. Where *could* the brownie be?

It was most peculiar really. Mister Straws had looked in every corner, in every pail, in every churn. He had run his hand along every shelf, and had even climbed up to the rafters and looked there. But not a thing could he see. There was no brownie to be found anywhere.

'I told you there was a brownie about, didn't I?' said the old cow-woman, Dame Milky. 'And didn't I tell you to put down a saucer of cream for him each night, so that he wouldn't get into the dairy and plague you? Ah, I know the ways of those brownies, I do. A saucer of cream, and they'll leave you alone – but neglect them, and they'll play you some fine tricks.'

'What I can't understand is where he hides!' said the farmer, scratching his head. 'I've looked everywhere!'

'Yes, it's a puzzle,' said Dame Milky. 'I've looked too - but I can't see him either - and all the time you hear that wicked little chuckle of his - ah, I'd like to get my hands on the little rogue, so I would! Master, why not go to Mother Buttercup and ask her to look for the Brownie with those sharp eyes of hers? She's a rare one for seeing.'

So Farmer Straws went off to Mother Buttercup and begged her to come and tell him where the brownie was hiding. She came at once, and peered round with her little sharp eyes. As she looked, a small chuckle sounded from some-where. Mother Buttercup looked about at once - and then she nodded her head and turned to the Farmer.

'You won't ever find that Brownie,' she said. 'He can't be seen! He's invisible! He must have drunk some magic drink that makes him unseeable. Aha, Farmer Straws, he'll be there for the rest of his

118

life and yours, tormenting you, and plaguing you! Why didn't you set down a saucer of cream for him as Dame Milky told you to? He would have been satisfied with that!'

She went off – and the farmer sat down on a stool and groaned in despair. It was bad enough having a brownie teasing him – but to have one that could never be caught because he couldn't be seen was worse still! If only he could get hold of him to give him one good slap!

'Aha!' said a small voice nearby, and that little brownie chuckle came again.

The farmer turned – but, of course, he could see nothing at all.

He went to the farmhouse to his tea. His two children were there, sharp little monkeys, called Jack and Rosy. They saw their father looking gloomy and they asked him what was the matter. So he told them, with much shaking of his head.

'He's ruining me!' he groaned. 'The milk, cream, butter and cheese I have to throw away each day! You see, the brownie turns it sour when he touches it. It's no use for anything. Well, if this goes on, children, you won't either of you get those ponies you've been wanting!'

'Father! But you promised!' said the two children in dismay.

'Well, you think of some way to get hold of this brownie, my dears, and you can have your ponies!' said Farmer Straws, and off he went to feed his pigs.

'Father! Father! Will you promise to let us have our ponies if we get the brownie for you?' Jack called after him.

121

'All right!' shouted back the farmer, and went into the pig-sties.

'*We* can't catch that brownie!' said Rosy, to Jack. 'If anyone could it would be old Mother Buttercup or Dame Milky – but *they* haven't done so!'

'Just wait a minute,' said Jack, his eyes gleaming. 'I've got an idea. I'm going shopping. Coming?'

Off they went. Jack went to the chemist and got five pence worth of snuff, or sneezing-powder. Then he went to buy himself and Rosy a pair of stout gardening gloves. Rosy could not think what he was doing!

'Wait and see!' chuckled Jack. 'I've got a fine plan!'

That evening, when the milking was done, and the cream was set out in bowls in the dairy, the two children crept in at the door.

'Shut all the windows,' said Jack, 'and I'll lock the door.'

This was done. Then Jack told Rosy to put on her pair of thick gardening gloves, and he slipped his on too. From

somewhere in the dairy came a tiny chuckle. Jack heard it.

'All right, my fine fellow!' he called. 'I can hear you! You'll be caught in a minute!'

There came the sound of a louder chuckle and Jack grinned. No wonder that brownie had angered his father!

Get out your handkerchief, Rosy,' whispered Jack. 'Hold it over your mouth. I am going to blow this sneezing powder into every corner of the dairy – and then, my word, we'll have that brownie in our hands before we can say "Jack Robinson".'

Rosy held her handkerchief to her mouth. Jack took out the box of snuff and began to blow it into every corner.

And soon he heard the sound he wanted to hear. 'A-tishoo! A-tishoo!'

'He's over there! said Jack, and the two children rushed to the far corner. But the brownie slipped between their legs, and got away.

'A-tishoo! A-tishoo!' he sneezed, and again the two children rushed to the place where the sneezing came from. But once more the brownie escaped. The children could not see him, but the sneezing was so loud that they could always guess where he was as soon as he sneezed.

'A-tishoo! A-tishoo! A-tishoo!' sneezed the brownie, trying his best to stop his sneezing – but the more he tried, the worse it got! 'A-tishoo! A-tishoo!'

'Over there by the milk-churn!' cried Rosy, and off went the two children. They felt the brownie slip by them, and very nearly caught him that time.

'He's very small!' said Jack. 'We must put our hands down to get him next time.

Jack blew out some more of the sneezing-powder, and at once they heard the brownie sneezing without stopping! 'A-tishoo! A-tishoo! A-tishoo! A-tishoo!'

'Over there!' shouted Jack, and the two children ran to the corner where the sneezing came from. Both put their hands down – and caught hold of a small wriggling body!

'Got him!' cried Rosy. 'Hurrah!'

The brownie began to bite and scratch for all he was worth. Rosy was glad that Jack had thought of buying thick gardening gloves. She shook the naughty little creature hard, and cried: 'Now behave yourself! Let us see you, and maybe we'll bargain with you, and let you go!'

The brownie suddenly became still in their hands, and they looked down. He was beginning to be visible! He was gradually appearing before them. First his pointed, cheeky face, then his long arms, then his rounded body, and last of all his short, knobby legs. There he was – the wicked little brownie, grinning up at them, and once more trying to wriggle out of their hands.

'Let me go!' he said.

'Not till we've had a talk!' said Jack firmly.

'Now listen to me. We've got you, and if we hand you over to our father, you will get such a spanking! My, I wouldn't like to be you!'

127

'No, no, don't do that!' begged the brownie, really frightened. 'Let me go. I promise I won't plague your father any more. Just put down a saucer of cream for me each night, and I'll be good. I won't put so much as one eyelash into the dairy, I promise you!'

'No, not one saucer of cream do you get!' said Jack. 'You'll go right away from here, and you'll never come back! If you ever come around here again, I'll use my sneezing-powder, and hand you over to our father at once. I promise you that!'

'Just a little saucer of cream each night!' wailed the brownie.

'Oh, if you're going to be a nuisance, we'll give you to father straightaway,' said Rosy, and she made as if she were going to take the brownie out to the pigsties. He screamed and kicked, and tried to bite through her glove.

'That's enough!' said Jack sharply, and he gave the brownie a slap.

'I'll do all you say, I will, I will!' wept the naughty little creature. 'I'll go this very minute!'

129

'Off you go then!' said Jack, and he let the brownie slip from his hands. The small creature hopped out into the farm-yard, and looked about to see which way to go. The farmer, coming out from his pig-sties, saw him, and shook his fist at him.

'Same to you, same to you!' yelled the defiant brownie, and made a rude face at Mister Straws, who was too far away to get him.

But the farmer's dog saw him, and he came after the brownie with a loud bark. 'Wuff! Wuff!'

'Ooooooooweeeee!' shrieked the little fellow in dismay, and hopped up on the wall. He ran along it, leapt into a bush, and disappeared – and that was the last they saw of that tiresome brownie!

'How did you find him?' Farmer Straws cried.

The children ran up and told him. Farmer Straws slapped his knee and roared when he heard about the sneezing-powder.

'A pretty trick, a pretty trick!' he shouted. 'Well my clever ones, if that brownie leaves my dairy alone tonight, you shall have your ponies!'

The cream, butter and cheese were all untouched that night – so the children got their ponies, and very proud of them they are too!

As for the brownie, goodness knows where he went. If he should ever come to you remember this – put a saucer of cream down for him each night, and he'll play you no tricks – but if you forget you'll soon long to spank that tiresome brownie!

12

The Easter Chickens

Tommy was staying with Auntie Susan and Uncle Ben at the farm for Easter. Mummy and Daddy had gone away for a holiday by themselves, and Tommy was sorry because he did so like Easter at home. There were coloured Easter eggs on the breakfast table to eat then – and chocolate ones too – and perhaps a fluffy yellow chick tied to one egg, or a little rabbit.

'I don't expect Auntie Susan or Uncle Ben know what a little boy likes at

Easter,' thought Tommy. 'I don't expect they will buy me any eggs at all. I wish I was at home with Mummy and Daddy!'

Sure enough, when Easter morning came and Tommy ran downstairs to breakfast, there was no coloured egg for him in his egg-cup – only just an ordinary brown egg laid by Henny-Penny, the brown hen.

Tommy looked to see if there were any chocolate eggs for him – but there wasn't even a very small one. He felt very sad.

'Sit down and eat your breakfast, Tommy,' said Auntie Susan. 'We must

get on because I have a lot of things to do today.' Auntie Susan always had a lot of things to do. So did Uncle Ben. Perhaps that was why they hadn't remembered his Easter eggs, Tommy thought. He remembered how he had seen a little yellow chick in the sweet shop yesterday down in the village. It was carrying an egg. He would have liked that very much. He wondered if he should ask Auntie Susan if she would buy it for him, but he decided not to. Mummy had always said that he mustn't ask for things. She said if he was nice enough, people would always buy him things because they loved him without being asked.

'I may not have been nice enough,' Tommy thought. So, instead of being sulky and disappointed, he tried to be extra nice to Auntie Susan, and ate his egg without dropping a single bit of the yellow part on the tablecloth.

'Can I go on any errands for you, Auntie Susan?' he asked, when he had finished breakfast.

'I think Uncle Ben wants you to go down to the hen-coops with him,' said Auntie. 'I'm coming too.'

So they all three went down to the hen-coops. There were four of these, with four brown hens sitting on thirteen eggs each.

And do you know, when they came to the first hen-coop, some of the eggs had hatched! Yes – and there were three yellow chicks running about saying: 'Cheep-cheep-cheep!' as loudly as they could.

'Oh!' said Tommy, delighted. 'Look at those dear little chicks, Auntie! Do look at them! They are much sweeter than the toy ones I saw in the shop yesterday! And oh, look – they have got something tied to their backs – whatever are they carrying?'

'Look and see,' said Uncle Ben with a laugh.

So Tommy crouched down and peeped to see what they were carrying. The chicks had gone into the coop with their mother and it was difficult to see one.

At last one of them came out again – and what *do* you suppose it had got on its back? A little chocolate egg! Fancy that!

'It's carrying an egg, just like the little chick at the sweet shop!' cried Tommy. 'Oh, who is the egg for, Auntie Susan?'

'It's for a nice little boy I know, called Tommy,' said Auntie Susan, laughing. 'That chick has an egg from *me*, Tommy – and that one has an egg for you from Uncle Ben – and the third one has an egg from Mummy and Daddy. It came for you yesterday, and we kept it till Easter Day. Then when the chicks hatched out, we thought you would like to have eggs and chicks together – really proper Easter chicks this time!'

'Auntie! Are the yellow chicks for me as well?' Oh I am *so* pleased!'

Uncle Ben caught the chicks and took off the chocolate eggs for Tommy. The little boy cuddled the soft cheeping chicks. Their little bodies were so warm. He loved the tiny creatures – and they were his very own!

'Will they grow into hens and lay me eggs?' he asked.

'Oh yes!' said Auntie Susan. 'You shall take them home with you next week when you go – real, live Easter chicks, Tommy for your very own!'

'This is the nicest Easter I've ever

had,' said Tommy. 'And I thought it wasn't going to be. What *will* Mummy say when I take home my Easter chicks!'

Tommy still has his chicks – but they are growing into brown hens now and will soon lay him eggs – one for his own breakfast each morning, one for his Mummy, and one for his Daddy. Don't you think he is lucky?

13

Annabelle's Little Thimble

Annabelle had a nice little work-basket that Granny had given her. You should have seen it! There were needles of all sizes, a bright pair of scissors, black, white, grey, green and blue cottons, and a pin-cushion. But best and brightest of all was Annabelle's little silver thimble.

Mummy had given it to her on her birthday. It was made of real silver, so it fitted Annabelle's middle finger beautifully, and she was very proud of it.

She took great care to keep her work-basket shut when Rascal the Jackdaw was about. He was a tame jackdaw that Daddy had picked up from the ground when he was a tiny bird, fallen from the nest. Daddy had fed him and tamed him and now he hopped and flew around the house, and loved to talk to anyone he met.

But he was so fond of bright things
that everyone was careful not to leave
any spoons, brooches, necklaces or
silver pencils about. If they did Rascal
the Jackdaw would take them and hide
them away in one of his cubby-holes in
the garden. Once Daddy had found a
whole collection of things tucked away
in a corner of the potting-shed – a pair of
scissors, two spoons from next door,
some pieces of silver paper and a little
gilt pin!

Rascal couldn't help taking them
because he was so fond of shiny things.
Daddy had often smacked him on the
beak for going off with things, but it
didn't cure him! So everyone had to be
very careful not to leave glittering
things about.

Annabelle had always been careful of
her little thimble, because she had seen
Rascal looking at it two or three times,
when she put it on her finger. But there
came a morning when she forgot.

She was sewing a new bonnet for her
doll when Mummy called her 'Quick,

Annabelle! There's Auntie Sue!'

Annabelle loved Auntie Sue so she hurriedly put down her work, stuck her thimble on top of it and ran to meet her Auntie.

And as soon as she was safely out of the door Rascal the Jackdaw came in at the window! He spied the bright little thimble at once and pounced on it. Ah! He had wanted that for ever so long. Where should he put it?

He went and sat on the kitchen window-sill, holding it in his beak. Cook was busy making Christmas puddings, and she didn't even look at him. Rascal watched her. Dear me, cook had lots of bright things too, on the table beside her!

Yes – she had six one pence pieces, four five pence pieces, a very small silver elephant, a tiny silver doll, a little silver horseshoe and one big, bright twenty pence. She was going to put them in the Christmas pudding for luck! It was always fun at Christmas time to see who got the treasures out of the pudding.

Rascal watched cook drop the shining things into the pudding. He thought cook was hiding them. What a good place to hide them! He waited until Cook went to the cupboard to get something and then he hopped to the table. He dropped Annabelle's silver thimble into the sticky mixture and then covered it neatly up with the currants and chopped nuts in the dish. Ha! It was a splendid hiding place!

145

But oh dear me, what a to-do when Annabelle ran to get her sewing again! Where was her dear little silver thimble? Gone! Nowhere to be found at all! Everyone hunted all over the place, but it couldn't be found.

'Rascal must have taken it,' said poor Annabelle in tears. So Daddy went to look in all the hidey-holes he knew the jackdaw had. But they were empty. Not one of them had Annabelle's thimble in it.

Annabelle was very unhappy. She did so like her thimble, and besides Mummy had given it to her. It was dreadful to lose something Mummy had bought for her. No other thimble would be half so nice!

'Perhaps someone will give you another one at Christmas time,' said Mummy, kissing her.

'It won't be as nice as the one *you* gave me, Mummy!' said Annabelle. 'It helped me sew so nicely. I shan't sew so well with any other thimble, I'm sure!'

'Rubbish!' said Mummy, smiling. She

made up her mind to ask Annabelle's Auntie Sue to give the little girl another thimble for Christmas. Mummy wanted to give Annabelle a new doll. Auntie Sue promised Mummy she would buy a lovely new thimble for Annabelle.

But, you know, she forgot about it! Yes, she bought Annabelle a fairy-tale book instead – so when Christmas came there was no silver thimble for Annabelle! She was so disappointed. But she didn't say anything, of course. She loved all her presents very much, especially her new doll – but she *would* have liked a new thimble!

Christmas dinnertime came. What a big turkey there was – and what a lot of people to eat it! Granny and Grandpa, three aunties, two uncles and Cousin Jane and Cousin Jimmy as well as Annabelle herself and Mummy and Daddy. But there was quite enough for everybody!

Then Cook brought in the Christmas pudding with a bit of holly stuck on top. How the children clapped their hands! What a splendid pudding it looked!

'Hope I get a five pence!' cried Cousin Jane.

148

'Hope I get a twenty pence!' cried Cousin Jimmy.

'And I hope I get the little silver elephant!' cried Annabelle. Everyone was served, and then what a hunt there was through the pieces of pudding to see if anyone had been lucky.

'A five pence for me!' cried Daddy. 'Hurrah!'

'Twenty pence for me!' cried Cousin Jimmy fishing out a twenty pence from his piece of pudding.

'What have *I* got?' cried Annabelle, feeling her spoon scrape against something hard. She looked at the treasure *she* had and then she cried out in astonishment.

'Mummy! Daddy! It's my own little silver thimble that I lost ages ago! Oh, look! How did it come in the pudding? Oh, it's my own dear little thimble!'

Mummy and Daddy *were* surprised! Annabelle ran out to ask Cook if she knew it had been put in the pudding, but Cook didn't know anything about it at all!

'I expect it's a little trick Santa Claus played on you!' she said.

'Caw, caw, caw!' suddenly said a loud voice, and Rascal the Jackdaw looked in at the window.

'Oh, Rascal, I wonder if *you* took my thimble and dropped it into the pudding!' cried Annabelle. 'Did you, Rascal?'

'Caw, caw, caw!' said the jackdaw. And Annabelle didn't know whether he meant yes or no! But she didn't mind; she had got back her little silver thimble after all. It was the nicest Christmas surprise she had had!

14

The Poor Little Owl

In the field nearby lived a little brown owl. John and Betty often saw it sitting on the telegraph wires in the dusk, when they went to bed.

'Tvit, tvit, tvit!' said the little owl to them, and the children called 'Tvit, tvit!' back to it. It wasn't very big, and when it spread its wings it flew very silently indeed.

Then one evening, as John and Betty walked home, they saw the little owl disappear into a hole in an old, old willow tree.

'I guess it has got its nest there!' said John in excitement. 'I wonder if there will be any baby owls. We must watch and see.'

But before they knew, a sad thing happened to the little owl. It went to drink from the pond one night, overbalanced, fell into the water and couldn't get out! So in the morning John and Betty found that it was drowned, and they were very sad.

'Oh, John – what about the baby owls, if there are any in the tree?' said Betty in tears. 'There won't be anyone to feed them. They will starve to death, poor things.

John spoke to the gardener about the owl's nest which he was sure was in the old willow tree. 'Couldn't you look and see if there are any baby owls there?' he said. 'We don't want them to starve, you know.'

'I'm not going after any owls,' said the gardener at once. 'Dangerous creatures they are, with their sharp claws! My goodness, even a baby owl

The Poor Little Owl

can get its claws into you so hard that you can't get them out.'

'Oh,' said John. He went away, but he kept on and on thinking about the owls. He felt sure they were hungry and unhappy.

'Betty, there must be some way of getting them out,' he said. 'Do think. You're clever at thinking.'

So Betty thought. 'Well,' she said, 'if their claws are so sharp and strong that they can dig right into your hand

153

and not let it go, what about letting down something into the nest – a handkerchief, perhaps – and letting them dig their claws into that. Then all we need to do is to draw up the handkerchief and the owls will come too!'

'Marvellous idea!' cried John. And so it was. Betty borrowed a big old silk hanky from Father's drawer, and the two children went to the old willow tree. They climbed up it and came to the hole, which went deep into a thick branch of the tree.

A faint hissing noise came up from the hole. 'Goodness – is there a snake in there?' said Betty.

'No! Owls do hiss, you know,' said John. 'Now, Betty – where's the hanky? Hand it over.'

John took the hanky and let one end slowly down into the hole. There were two baby owls in the tree. They turned themselves over so that their clawed feet were on top – and how they attacked that silk hanky! They dug

The Poor Little Owl

their feet into it and their claws caught in the silk.

'Got them – it worked!' shouted John, and he pulled up the hanky. There were the two fluffy baby owls holding on to it for all they were worth! John popped them into a box he had brought with him, shut the lid, and then switched his torch on to see the nest.

'There isn't really any nest,' he called to Betty, 'just a few shavings from the hole, that's all. But wait a minute – what's this?'

The light of his torch had shone on to something red. John put his hand into the hole and felt what it was. It seemed

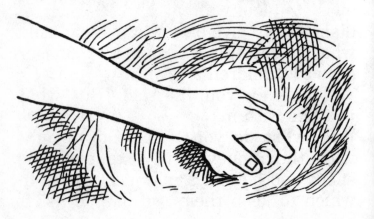

to be a little bag of some sort. He pulled at it – and it came out. It was heavy.

'Betty! The owl had made her nest on top of this little bag!' cried John. 'Look – it's got the name of the bank on it. I do believe it's the diamonds that a thief stole from the bank last winter! He must have hidden it here and then forgotten where the hiding-place was!'

'Goodness!' said Betty, as John opened the little red bag and a whole heap of shining diamonds winked up at them. 'What a lot of diamonds! Come and tell Mummy.'

Well, that was a most exciting afternoon. The children had two baby owls to look after, and a bag of diamonds to give back to the bank! And what do you think? The bank manager gave the children a reward!

'That's for you,' he said. 'Buy what you like with it.'

So what do you think they bought with the money? They went to the shops and bought a marvellous cage in which to keep their two baby owls! It was strong wire mesh outside, and had wooden perches inside, and was very grand and big indeed.

'You can keep your little owls there and bring them up in safety till they are

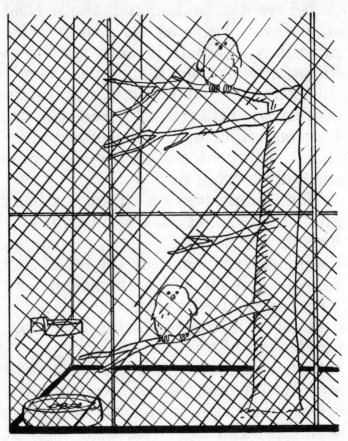

big enough to fly away and look after themselves,' said their mother. 'You must feed them well, give them fresh water, and clean out their cage every single day.'

So they did, and soon the two owls grew used to Betty and John and would sit quietly on their perches while the children were feeding them and cleaning out their cage. Betty and John were very proud of them, because no one else at school had owls; and even the teacher came to see them, and said what strange and curious birds they were.

'They look rather like little feathered cats!' she said. And so they did, as they sat side by side on their perches, their big golden eyes looking solemnly at the visitor.

And now they have flown away to look after themselves; but John and Betty have left the cage door open in case they might like to come back there to sleep. I expect they will sometimes.

Every night the two little birds call to their friends and say 'Tvit, tvit, tvit!'

from the nearby field. I wonder if you have heard them. They call so sharply and so loudly that I shouldn't be a bit surprised if you hear them too!

15

The Banana Robber

John, Sheila and Mollie had a playroom up in the attic and they played there on rainy days. Mother let them have tea up there sometimes, and that was great fun. They carried up their mugs, plates, a jug of milk, three slices of cake and some apples or bananas. They were all very fond of fruit, and used to spend half their pocket-money on it and store it in the playroom cupboard.

One day Uncle Jim gave John fifty pence and he showed it to the others.

'I know what we'll do,' he said. 'I'll buy bananas with it, and we'll pretend we are cast on a lonely island where banana trees grow, and we'll eat them because there is nothing else and we might starve!'

'That would be a fine game to play,' said the two girls. 'Let's make some trees and tie the bananas on them.' So they borrowed poles from the potting-shed and nailed leafy twigs on them for branches. They put them here and there in their playroom, and emptied some sand from their sand-tray on the floor to make believe that it was the sandy shore of an island.

'The table upside down can be our boat,' said John. 'What fun we'll have! I'll be captain. Sheila, can you tie some bananas on this tree, and Mollie and I will do the others? There are fourteen bananas so we will be able to play this game two or three times before they are all eaten!'

162

Before they had finished getting things ready it was bedtime. The trees had their bananas on and looked fine. The table had the cloth for a sail and the floor was chalked with blue to make it look like the sea.

'We'll play the game tomorrow,' said John, and off they went to bed.

After tea the next day the three raced up to the playroom. There was the table, all ready to be a boat. There were the trees, all ready with their bananas. What fun!

'Now this table had better be a lifeboat, or a raft,' said John. 'Get in, you girls. We're escaping from a wrecked ship!'

They all got in. John swayed about as if the boat was rocking up and down on the sea. 'Hold on tight!' he shouted. 'I see land! Land ahoy! A lonely island! The tide is taking us there! Be ready to jump.'

The girls screamed, and swayed about like John, pretending that the boat was rocked up and down. 'Now

then!' cried John, 'we are near the beach. Jump! Jump for your lives!'

They all jumped out of the boat on to the sand. Sheila lay down as if she were tired out. John and Mollie took off their overalls and squeezed them, pretending they were wet through.

'I'm so hungry!' moaned Sheila, sitting up. 'We shall starve here. There is nothing to eat.'

'Look! Look! Banana trees, with real bananas growing on them!' shouted John, jumping to his feet. 'Come and pick them.'

They went to the banana trees, and John gave a shout of surprise.

'I say! There are no bananas on my tree! Just look! Which of you girls has taken my bananas?'

'I haven't!' said Mollie. 'And I haven't!' said Sheila.

'Well, they're gone,' said John. 'And look – there is the peel on the floor. Oh, I say – it's too bad. Someone's been up and taken three of my bananas. I wonder who it can be.'

'Well, they're eaten,' said Mollie. 'You'll have to share our tree, John!'

So they gave John two bananas off their trees – but the game was spoilt. It was so horrid to feel that someone had taken their bananas. It was such a mean trick.

'We'll play this game tomorrow,' said John. 'There are still some bananas left.'

Next evening after tea they raced upstairs again to their playroom, and the game began once more – but would you believe it, before they had jumped out of the boat on to the sandy shore, Mollie gave a shout. 'Look!' she said. 'There is some more peel on the floor. Someone has taken more of our bananas! Whoever can the robber be?'

'It's very strange,' said John, getting out of the boat and walking up to the peel thrown down on the floor. 'It's not any of us, that's certain, for we'd tell each other if it were. And it can't be anyone in the house, or we'd see them going up here!'

'Shall we hide behind the cupboard door and see if we can find out who the robber is?' cried Mollie. 'Do let's!'

'All right,' said John. 'Come on. Let's hide now. The robber might come any time.'

So, very quietly, they crouched behind the big cupboard door and peeped through the crack to watch who the robber might be. They waited a long time, but nobody came. John watched the door, and he kept thinking it was opening little by little, but it wasn't.

'I'm getting tired of this,' whispered Mollie. 'Let's go out, now, and play, John, shall we?'

'Perhaps we'd better,' said John. 'The banana robber isn't coming this evening!'

But even as he spoke, the three children heard a noise. They held their breaths and looked at the door. But nothing came round it. They heard the noise again – a little scraping sound – and it came from the window, not the door! The children peered through the crack. Who could it be at the window?

A strange little face looked in – a little brown face with bright, dark eyes. Then in at the window came – what do you think? Yes – a small monkey! He jumped in and ran to the trees stuck up here and there on the floor. He ran up one and pulled a banana down. He slid down to the floor with a little happy chattering sound. He peeled the banana and bit off a piece of the yellow fruit inside. Then he threw down the peel and went up the tree again!

'So that's the banana robber!' said John, and he ran out of the cupboard. 'Come on, you girls – this is a real desert island now with monkeys and everything! Hurrah!'

The monkey looked up in surprise. He seemed pleased to see John. He made a little chattering noise again and suddenly jumped right into John's arms! The little boy was startled, but very pleased to find the small monkey so friendly. He hugged him, and the two girls came up and stroked him.

'Let's take him downstairs and show Mummy,' said John. So down they went. Mummy was astonished.

'Why, he must be the monkey that Mrs. Bailey lost last week!' she said. 'He escaped and went up on the roof of her house, and then she lost sight of him. He must have lived up on the roofs for a few days – and seeing the bananas on your make-believe trees, he crept in to get them for food. You'd better take him back.'

So the children took him back to Mrs.

Bailey, and when she heard that he had stolen their bananas, what do you think she did? She gave them fifty pence to make up for the stolen bananas, and another fifty pence for bringing back the monkey.

'Now we can buy bananas, apples and oranges!' said John joyfully. And off they went to the greengrocer's. Weren't they lucky?

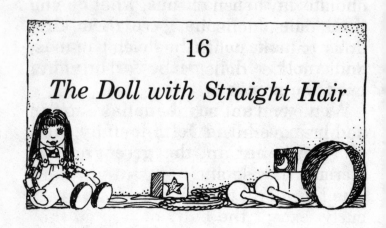

16
The Doll with Straight Hair

In the toy-shop there was every kind of toy you can think of – engines, motor-cars, dolls of all sorts, pandas, tops, ducks, dogs, pigs, dolls' houses – it was really a perfectly lovely place! All the children went there to spend their Saturday pocket money, and on birth-days and before Christmas mothers and fathers and uncles and aunts bought hundreds of exciting things in the shop.

172

The Doll with Straight Hair

On one shelf sat the dolls. You should have seen them! Big dolls and little dolls, dolls in blue frocks, and dolls in red, white or yellow: sailor dolls, soldier dolls, baby dolls, grown-up dolls; scores of them!

At the end sat a little doll dressed in a blue overall. All the other dolls laughed at her, and do you know why? It was because she had straight hair! The hair of all the other dolls was very curly, except the baby dolls, and they had no hair at all!

'Nowadays it is not the thing to have straight hair,' said the golden-haired doll scornfully. 'You do look queer!'

'Even the golliwog has a nice curly wave in his black hair,' said a sailor doll.

'And as for us,' said two little black dolls, 'you couldn't put a pin in our hair without running it through a tight little curl!'

They certainly had curly heads. The little doll in the blue overall looked at them with envy. How she did wish she had curly hair, too!

'You'll never be sold,' said the soldier doll. 'You'll be left on the shelf long after we have all gone to lovely homes to be played with by nice little girls and boys.'

'I wish I could get my hair curled,' said the little doll in the blue overall, with tears in her eyes.

'Well, you can't,' said the golden-haired doll. 'It's terribly straight! I never did see such very straight hair in my life!'

'Sssshhh!' whispered the golliwog. 'There is someone coming into the shop. It's an uncle, I think!'

A big man came into the shop and the shop-girl hurried to serve him. He looked at the dolls, and the girl took down the golden-haired one and another with dark curls down her back.

'I'll take those,' said the man. 'They have such pretty hair – and I know my little niece will love them!'

Off he went with the parcel, and the toys turned to the little doll in the blue

174

overall.

'What did we tell you?' they said. 'You will never get sold with that straight hair of yours!'

Now that night the little doll was very unhappy. She sat and thought and thought at the end of the shelf. Whatever could she do to get curly hair?

Then she remembered that once she had seen the shop-girl open a big drawer under the counter – and in it had been a great many dolls' wigs – brown ones, golden ones and red ones. The girl sold them for dolls whose hair had come off or got thin. The wigs were stuck on to the dolls' heads and then they looked as fine as ever again. Suppose the little doll went to the drawer and got a new curly wig for herself? She could put it on over her straight hair – and then she would look fine, and might be sold to a nice little girl.

So she slipped off her shelf and went to the drawer. It was open the tiniest bit. The little doll squeezed herself into it and began to hunt about among the wigs. She found one that seemed very curly indeed, and fitted it on to her head.

And then, just at that moment, she heard someone coming into the shop! It was the man who owned the shop. The shop-girl had gone hours ago. The man

had come to look for something. He hunted round, found what he wanted, and was just going out when he caught sight of the drawer under the counter.

'How many times have I told that girl to keep the drawer shut?' he said crossly. 'We shall get mice making their nests in the dolls' wigs again!'

He shut the drawer with a bang! And inside lay the little doll in the blue overall, frightened out of her life! She couldn't get out! She was in the dark! Oh dear, oh dear, this was a dreadful punishment for her because she had been naughty enough to think of getting a curly wig for herself!

She cried tears all over the wigs. She pushed against the drawer, but it wouldn't open at all. She must just stay there, frightened and alone till someone found her.

She fell asleep on the wigs. She

178

awoke next day and heard people coming in and out of the shop. And then she heard a little girl's soft voice.

'I have come to choose something for my birthday. I think I will have a doll. Have you got one with straight hair like mine? All my dolls have curly hair, and I felt as if I would like a little doll that was like me. I would feel she was really my own little girl then.'

The doll in the drawer could have cried with despair! However could she get out? The shop-girl looked at the shelf of dolls and took some down. 'These are all we have,' she said. 'They all seem to have curly hair. Not one has straight hair! Dolls always have curly hair now, you know.'

'I know,' said the little girl. 'But it is so difficult to comb, you see. I couldn't tell you how many combs I've broken trying to comb out the tangles in my dolls' hair! Oh, dear, I did so want a straight-haired doll. Haven't you a straight-haired wig, please, that I could let a doll wear?'

179

'No, I don't think so,' said the shop-girl. She pulled open the wig drawer – and the little doll in the blue overall popped up her head and beamed all over her face as if to say 'Here I am!'

The little girl gave a scream of delight and took the doll up at once.

'She's got straight hair – and brown eyes like me – and she wears a blue overall like I do! Oh, oh, I must have this dear darling little doll!'

'I can't think how she got into the drawer,' said the girl, puzzled. 'She is two pounds, miss. You can have her cheap, because she's got straight hair.'

'Oh, I love her!' said the little girl in delight. She paid two pounds and went out of the shop carrying the doll in her arms, both of them as happy as can be.

'Well,' said the golliwog in surprise, 'it doesn't do to think that curly hair and silk frocks are always better than straight hair and blue overalls! I guess that little doll will be happier than any of us!'

And, you know, she was!

The Doll with Straight Hair

181

17

The Lost Baby Mouse

There was once a little mouse who was far too daring. He ran out of his hole at any time of the day or night, and his mother was very cross with him.

'One of these days you will get caught by the cat,' she said.

'Oh, I'm too quick for the cat!' the little mouse said, and he twitched his whiskers to and fro in a way that made his mother very angry.

'Don't make faces at me!' she cried, crossly. The little mouse gave a squeak and ran right out of his hole. Luckily for him the cat was not there, or that would have been the end of him. The hole led out into the kitchen, and there were often crumbs and scraps of food to be found on the floor.

The little mouse hunted round for some, but there were none because they had all been swept up. 'Well, I'll look round the world a bit and see what I can find somewhere else,' thought the little mouse. So he ran out of the kitchen door into the hall.

He came to the stairs. He saw the first step – and the second step – and the third step – good gracious, it seemed to him as if these enormous stairs must lead up to the sky!

'Now I've heard that the moon is

made of green cheese,' said the baby mouse to himself, 'and if so it would be a wonderful place to live. These great big steps must surely lead up to the moon. Tails and whiskers, how high up they go!'

The mouse began to climb them one by one. It seemed a very long way up to him. But at last he reached the very, very top. There was a landing at the top, and four or five doors led off it. The mouse ran into the nearest one.

It was the playroom where the children had all their toys, and played happily together. The mouse was very frightened to see a bear, a horse, a dog, an elephant, and a pink rabbit staring at him.

'Oh, pardon me!' he said, trying to back out of the door quickly. 'I didn't know this was the zoo.'

The teddy bear laughed so much that he couldn't speak. So the pink rabbit spoke up.

'Of course it's not the zoo, silly. We are only toys.'

184

But the mouse had gone in a fright. He ran to another door. A bedroom was behind that, cold and empty. All the other doors were shut.

And then the cat appeared! My goodness! It came stalking round the corner of the landing, tail in the air, green eyes gleaming!

The mouse gave a squeak of fright. He ran into the playroom, with the cat after him. The cat pounced – and the baby mouse's tail was scratched by the cat's big claws. It dashed into an open brick-box and the teddy bear neatly shut the lid on him!

'Sssss!' hissed the cat at the bear.

But she didn't like his staring glass eyes and she turned and went out of the door again.

'She's gone,' said the bear, opening the box. 'Are you hurt, Baby Mouse?'

'My tail is bleeding,' wept the poor little creature. 'Oh, whatever am I to do? I am quite, quite lost. I was looking for the moon up here to have a good feast of green cheese – but it didn't seem to be anywhere.'

'You won't find the moon up here, Baby Mouse. Hasn't your mother ever told you about the playroom? We see her sometimes when the children take us downstairs,' said the pink rabbit kindly. 'I say, where's Angela the doll? She knows how to put bandages on. Angela! Come over here and see to this dear little mouse.'

Angela came up. She was a beautiful blue-eyed doll, with thick curly hair. She loved the tiny mouse as soon as she saw him. She made the pink rabbit fetch some water out of the goldfish bowl on the bookshelf to bathe the mouse's tail.

He climbed up with a dish out of the doll's-house, and soon came back carrying the water very carefully.

'Good rabbit,' said Angela. 'Put the bowl down there. Get the sponge out of the doll's-house bathroom.'

There was the tiniest sponge imaginable in the bathroom, and the rabbit fetched it. Soon Angela was bathing the mouse's tail. Then she tore her tiny white handkerchief in half and bound it neatly round the little tail.

'Oh, thank you,' said the mouse, gratefully. 'I do think you are kind. What shall I do now? Is there a mouse-hole anywhere in this playroom? I could go down it and live there. I shall never, never dare to go out of this room in case I meet the cat.'

'Well, there isn't a mouse-hole,' said the pink rabbit. 'We've often and often looked, little mouse. I suppose you wouldn't like to live in the brick-box?'

'No, thank you,' said the mouse. 'It's not very comfortable – and the children might tip me out with the bricks.'

'True,' said the bear. All the toys thought hard – and then the pink rabbit gave a squeal and clapped his fat paws together.

'I know!' he cried. 'Why can't the baby mouse live in the doll's-house? Nobody lives there at all, because the children took all the little dolls out to live in the toy farmyard and look after the animals there. The baby mouse is just small enough.'

'Oh, that is a good idea!' cried

everyone. 'Come along, Mouse – we'll take you in at the front door.'

So they all trooped across to the doll's-house, and the teddy knocked on the little brass knocker. Of course there was nobody to answer, so they just pushed open the door. Only the mouse was small enough to go in at the door, and he ran into the tiny hall in delight.

'Oh, it's lovely!' he cried. 'Really lovely! Look at the tiny stairs! Are there bedrooms above?'

'There is one bedroom and a tiny bathroom,' said the rabbit, looking in at the window. 'Here, Mouse, take the sponge and put it back again in the bathroom. And you can have a bath if you like.'

Well, the baby mouse had a wonderful time. He filled the bath with water by

turning on the tiny tap. He got into it
and washed with the bit of soap there.
He got out, stood on the teeny-weeny
bath-mat and dried himself with the
towel. He did feel nice and clean after
that.

'I feel dreadfully tired,' he called to
the toys, who were all peeping in at the
windows, watching the mouse with joy.
'Do you think I might sleep in this bed?
It's just big enough for me. Would it
matter if I got under the blankets, do
you think? I love to be cosy.'

'Oh, do get into the bed!' cried the
doll. 'I will put my arm in at the
window and tuck you up. You will look
really sweet.'

So the baby mouse got into the tiny
doll's bed, and the big doll put her arm
in through the open window and tucked
him up. Just his ears, pointed nose, and
whiskers showed above the sheet. He
shut his eyes and in half a minute he
was fast asleep.

All the toys came to peep at him,
even the old plush monkey who was so

bad-tempered that nobody liked playing with him. Everyone loved looking at the baby mouse asleep in the doll's tiny bed.

'He can live here as long as he likes,' said Angela the doll. 'He can have his meals in the kitchen off the little table. We will teach him good manners. He can keep the house clean, and sometimes, for a treat, he can cook us some tiny cakes on the stove. We've always wanted to use the doll's-house stove, but we are all too big to go inside the kitchen door! Next time the children take me downstairs, I will tell his

191

mother that he is quite safe with us.'

So the baby mouse lived in the doll's-house, and felt quite safe there if the cat happened to come into the playroom. Once the cat came and looked in at the doll's-house window, and the mouse sat on the kitchen table and made faces at her. Angela said he shouldn't have done that because it was bad manners.

'But I did so like making faces at the cat,' said the mouse. 'Really I did. Oh, toys, I'm so glad I came to your playroom. I do so love my little house. The only thing is – how I wish one of you was small enough to come and have tea with me!'

And now the little mouse has got his wish! A clockwork mouse has come to live with the toys – and today the real mouse is having the clockwork mouse to tea! Wouldn't you love to peep in at a window and see them both sitting in the kitchen together? I would!